BORN TO RULE

TRUTH CAN WIN ANY BATTLE

MISS VASHISHTH

To my family and friends, whose love and strength inspire
me every day, and to those who rise above challenges to
find their true place in the world—this story of courage,
heart, and redemption is for you.

Contents

Foreword	*vii*
Preface	*ix*
Acknowledgements	*xi*
Prologue	*xiii*
1. A Love By The River	1
2. The Seeds Of Envy	7
3. A Child Of The Jungle	12
4. Shadows Of Udaipur	17
5. A Fateful Encounter	22
6. A Kingdom's Sorrow	27
7. A Murder's Shadow	32
8. The Twin's Truth	37
9. The War Of Brothers	42
10. A New Dawn	47

Foreword

Every kingdom has its stories—tales of kings and queens, of love that defies rules, and of secrets that shape destinies. *Born to Rule* is one such story, born from the heart of a world where palaces stand tall, jungles whisper mysteries, and the human spirit fights to rise above pain and betrayal.

This novel takes you to the vibrant kingdoms of Bhaanugarh, Udaipur, and Rajgarh, where a fisherwoman becomes a queen, a prince seeks justice, and a lost princess finds her way home. It's a journey of love that sparks by a river, of envy that tears families apart, and of courage that mends broken bonds. Through every twist—be it a stolen child, a false accusation, or a war between brothers—this story reminds us that true strength lies in the heart.

As you turn these pages, you'll walk through grand palaces and quiet fields, feel the weight of a crown and the warmth of a friend's hand. You'll meet characters who make mistakes, fight for redemption, and discover their purpose. This tale is for anyone who believes in love, who knows the sting of loss, and who dreams of a brighter tomorrow.

Welcome to *Born to Rule*. May its heroes inspire you, its heartaches teach you, and its triumphs lift your spirit.

PREFACE

When I began writing "Born to Rule", I wanted to tell a story that felt alive—a tale of kingdoms where love could bloom in the humblest places, where betrayal could break hearts, and where courage could mend them. Growing up, I was fascinated by stories of kings and queens, not just for their crowns but for their human struggles. What happens when a king falls in love with a fisherwoman? How does a princess, raised in a farmer's hut, find her way to a throne? These questions sparked this novel.

"Born to Rule" is set in the fictional lands of Bhaanugarh, Udaipur, and Rajgarh, where every character fights for their place in a world of loyalty and lies. It's about Anokhi, a girl of the fields who carries a royal heart; Nyay, a prince who seeks justice over power; and Adhirath, a king who learns the true meaning of family. Their journeys weave through love, loss, and battles, showing that destiny is shaped not by birth but by choices.

This story is my love letter to those who dare to dream beyond their circumstances, who face pain with bravery, and who find strength in forgiveness. As you read, I hope you feel the pulse of the palaces, the warmth of friendship, and the hope that shines through even the darkest moments. Thank you for joining me in this world.

Acknowledgements

Writing "Born to Rule" was a journey of heart and soul, and I could not have done it alone. My deepest thanks go to those who walked this path with me.

To my family, your endless love and belief in me gave me the courage to write this story. Your stories of strength and kindness inspired characters like Anokhi and Nyay. To my friends, thank you for listening to my ideas, cheering me on during late nights, and reminding me to keep going when the words felt heavy.

I'm grateful to my teachers and mentors, who taught me the power of stories and how to weave them with care. Your wisdom shaped this book. To the readers who shared their thoughts on early drafts, your feedback made this tale stronger and truer.

A special thank you to the vibrant culture and history of royal India, which breathed life into the kingdoms of Bhaanugarh, Udaipur, and Rajgarh. The music, colors, and traditions I grew up with are woven into every page.

Finally, to you, the reader, thank you for picking up this book. Your time and imagination bring Anokhi, Nyay, and their world to life. I hope their story touches your heart as much as it did mine.

PROLOGUE

The sun rose over Bhaanugarh, its golden rays kissing the marble domes of the grand palace. The kingdom buzzed with life—vendors shouted in the bustling market, children laughed by the river, and temple bells rang softly in the distance. At the heart of it all stood Raja Inderjeet Singh, a king loved by his people, his eyes warm but burdened with duty.

In the palace, silken curtains swayed in the breeze, and the scent of jasmine filled the air. Inderjeet sat on his throne, his royal turban gleaming with emeralds, listening to his advisors. But his mind wandered to a journey—a hunting trip by the river where he met her. Geetanjali, a fisherwoman with eyes like the morning sky, had stolen his heart. Her laughter echoed in his dreams, and her songs haunted the quiet nights.

He knew marrying her would stir whispers. His first wife, Rani Gayatri, was the pride of Bhaanugarh's nobility, her beauty matched only by her ambition. Yet, Inderjeet's heart chose Geetanjali, a woman of the river, not the court. He dreamed of a future where love ruled his kingdom, unaware of the storm it would unleash.

In the shadows, Gayatri watched, her heart heavy with envy. She had given Inderjeet loyalty but no heir, and now a new queen threatened her place. The palace, once a haven of joy, was about to become a battleground of love, betrayal, and secrets that would echo for generations.

I

A Love by the River

The forest near Bhaanugarh's river pulsed with life, a symphony of nature under a blazing midday sun. Birds trilled in the canopy, their songs weaving through the rustle of leaves stirred by a gentle breeze. The river sparkled like a ribbon of diamonds, its waters lapping against smooth pebbles. Raja Inderjeet Singh guided his white stallion through the towering trees, the soft crunch of hooves on the earth blending with the forest's hum. His royal guards trailed behind, their armor glinting like stars, but Inderjeet's heart was unburdened. These escapes from the palace were his sanctuary, a fleeting chance to shed the weight of his crown and breathe as a man, not a king.

He reined in his horse at the riverbank, the scent of wet moss and wild jasmine filling his lungs. His guards halted at a respectful distance, their murmurs fading. Inderjeet dismounted, his silk kurta shimmering with golden embroidery, and let the stallion graze. A soft, lilting voice floated over the water, a melody of love and distant stars that stopped him cold. It was unlike the polished songs of court musicians—raw, heartfelt, as if the river itself sang through her. Intrigued, he followed the sound, his boots sinking into the soft earth.

Beyond a cluster of reeds, he saw her. A young woman knelt by the river, her hands deftly weaving a fishing net, her fingers nimble as they danced over the coarse threads. Her dark hair cascaded over her shoulders, catching the sunlight like polished ebony, and her simple cotton sari clung to her frame, damp from the river's spray. Her eyes, when they lifted, held a quiet strength, like the calm before a storm. She was Geetanjali, a fisherwoman from a nearby village, and her beauty stole the breath from Inderjeet's chest.

"Beautiful song," he said, stepping forward, his voice warm but cautious, as if afraid to shatter the moment.

Geetanjali flinched, her net slipping from her hands into the shallow water. She stood quickly, brushing her palms on her sari, her gaze sharp. "Who are you, sneaking up like that?" Her voice was bold, tinged with defiance despite the surprise in her eyes.

Inderjeet smiled, charmed by her fire. "Just a traveler who loves music. I'm Inderjeet." He stepped closer, the river's edge lapping at his boots.

She raised an eyebrow, her lips twitching as she eyed his ornate kurta and the jeweled dagger at his waist. "Traveler, huh? Your clothes tell a different story." She crossed her arms, unyielding. "You're no wanderer."

He laughed, a rich sound that echoed off the water. "Alright, you caught me. I'm the king of Bhaanugarh. But today, I'm just a man who wants to hear you sing again."

Geetanjali's cheeks flushed, but she held his gaze, her eyes sparkling with mischief. "Sing for a king? My songs are for the river and the fish. I don't know if they're grand enough for a palace."

"They're grand enough for me," Inderjeet said softly, his voice carrying a sincerity that made her pause. He sat on a nearby rock, gesturing to the ground beside him. "Will you humor me, Geetanjali?"

She hesitated, then sat, her sari pooling around her. "How do you know my name?" she asked, narrowing her eyes.

"The village speaks of the girl who sings to the stars," he said, grinning. "I listen more than you think."

She laughed, a sound like temple bells, and began to sing again. Her voice wove a tale of a girl who loved a prince under a moonlit sky, her words painting dreams that danced across the river. Inderjeet listened, entranced, his heart swelling with a warmth he hadn't felt in years. When she finished, the silence felt sacred.

"That was…" he began, searching for words. "You make the world feel alive."

Geetanjali tucked a strand of hair behind her ear, shy now. "It's just a song. The river taught me."

"Then the river is a wise teacher," he said, leaning closer. "Tell me about your world, Geetanjali. What makes you sing like that?"

They talked for hours, the river their only witness. Geetanjali shared stories of her village—children chasing fireflies, her father's fishing boat, her mother's laughter before illness took her. Inderjeet spoke of Bhaanugarh's dreams, of a kingdom where every heart found peace, his voice earnest and unguarded. As the sun dipped low, painting the sky in hues of orange and pink, he knew he was falling in love. Her courage, her simplicity, her spirit—they were a melody he couldn't forget.

"Will you come to the palace?" he asked, his voice hesitant. "I want to see you again."

Geetanjali's eyes widened. "The palace? I'm a fisherwoman, Inderjeet. I don't belong there."

"You belong wherever your heart takes you," he said, taking her hand. "And mine is with you."

She pulled back, her smile fading. "You're a king. Your world has rules mine doesn't. What would your court say?"

"Let them talk," he said fiercely. "I'm not just a king. I'm a man who sees you."

The moment hung between them, fragile and electric. Geetanjali nodded slowly, her heart racing. "I'll think about it," she whispered, turning back to her net.

Inderjeet rode back to the palace, his mind ablaze with her face. The guards exchanged glances, sensing their king's joy. But in the palace, high on a balcony overlooking the kingdom, Rani Gayatri stood, her silk sari rustling in the evening breeze. Her emerald earrings caught the fading light, but her face was a mask of cold beauty. A guard approached, bowing low.

"My lady, the king lingered by the river," he reported. "He spoke with a woman—a fisherwoman named Geetanjali."

Gayatri's smile tightened, her fingers gripping the marble railing until her knuckles whitened. "A fisherwoman?" she murmured, her voice like ice. "He dares bring her here?" Her heart twisted, a storm of envy brewing within. She had been Bhaanugarh's pride, her beauty and grace unmatched, yet Inderjeet's eyes had never looked at her as they did today by the river.

"Find out everything about her," she ordered the guard, her voice low. "Every word, every step."

As the guard retreated, Gayatri turned to her chamber, where her maid, Kamla, waited. "He's smitten," Gayatri said, her voice trembling with rage. "A commoner, Kamla. How could he?"

Kamla's lips curled. "Men are fools for pretty faces, my lady. But faces fade. You are the queen."

"Not for long, if he has his way," Gayatri snapped, pacing. "I've given him loyalty, years of my life. And now this?"

Kamla stepped closer, her voice a whisper. "Then make sure she doesn't last. The court won't accept a fisherwoman. You know how to play their game."

Gayatri paused, her eyes narrowing. "Yes," she said slowly. "I do."

Days later, Inderjeet stood before his court, his voice steady but his heart pounding. "I will marry Geetanjali," he declared. The hall erupted in gasps, advisors whispering furiously. "She is my choice, and Bhaanugarh will honor her."

The wedding was a spectacle that lit up the kingdom. The palace was adorned with marigolds and jasmine, their scents mingling with the smoke of sacred fires. Geetanjali walked through the grand hall, her red lehenga shimmering with golden threads, her hands adorned with intricate henna designs. The people lined the streets, cheering, enchanted by her grace. Drummers played, and dancers swirled, their anklets jingling. Inderjeet stood at the altar, his royal turban gleaming with emeralds, his eyes locked on her.

"Welcome, my queen," he whispered, placing a pearl necklace around her neck, its luster pale against her radiance.

Geetanjali smiled, nervous but glowing. "I'm no queen, Inderjeet. Just a girl who loves you." Her voice trembled, the weight of the palace pressing on her.

"You're both," he said, kissing her hand, his touch a promise. The crowd roared, their joy a wave that crashed through the hall.

But in the shadows, Gayatri watched, her silk sari a dark contrast to the festive colors. Her heart burned, each cheer a dagger in her chest. She clutched a golden goblet, her fingers trembling. "Enjoy your throne, fisherwoman," she whispered to herself, her eyes cold as the night. "It won't be yours for long."

Kamla leaned in, her voice a hiss. "She's nothing, my lady. A passing fancy. You'll always be Bhaanugarh's true queen."

Gayatri's lips curved, but her smile held no warmth. "Oh, Kamla, she'll learn. The palace eats dreams like hers."

The halls echoed with music, the air alive with celebration, but beneath the joy, a storm was brewing. Geetanjali's new life as queen would test her heart, a fragile flame in a world of envy and ambition. Gayatri's bitterness, like a shadow, would set a tragic chain in motion, its echoes destined to shape Bhaanugarh for generations.

II
The Seeds of Envy

The palace of Bhaanugarh shimmered under a silver moon, its marble walls glowing like pearls in the night. Torches flickered along the corridors, casting dancing shadows on intricate carvings of elephants and lotuses. Inside, the air was thick with the scent of sandalwood and jasmine, and the faint strum of a sitar echoed from the courtyard. Geetanjali, the new queen, moved through the halls, her silk sari whispering against the polished floors. Her laughter, bright and unforced, filled the air as she knelt beside a group of servant children, their eyes wide with awe.

"Here, take these," she said, offering a handful of jalebis, their golden syrup glistening. A small girl with pigtails giggled, grabbing one. "Tell me, Rani-ji," she chirped, "do queens eat sweets too?"

Geetanjali's eyes sparkled. "This queen does, especially with friends like you." She sat cross-legged, listening as the children shared tales of their games by the river. The servants, once wary of a fisherwoman-turned-queen, now smiled warmly, calling her "Rani of the Heart" in hushed tones. Her kindness was a breeze that softened the palace's rigid air, but not all hearts welcomed it.

In her private chambers, Rani Gayatri sat before a golden mirror, its edges studded with rubies. Her sharp features, once the talk of Bhaanugarh's court, were taut with strain. Her maids brushed her long, ebony hair, but her mind was elsewhere, tangled in resentment. The distant sound of Geetanjali's laughter drifted through the window, each note a needle in Gayatri's heart. "They cheer for her," she muttered, her voice low and bitter, "as if I'm nothing."

Her closest confidante, Kamla, a cunning maid with sharp eyes, leaned in, her voice a conspiratorial whisper. "My lady, the people are fickle. They love her now, but they'll tire of her soon. A fisherwoman in silk? She's a passing fancy."

Gayatri's eyes narrowed, her reflection cold in the mirror. "She's no queen, Kamla. A fisherwoman in silk doesn't change her blood. I've given Inderjeet everything—my youth, my loyalty. And now this?"

Kamla's lips curled into a sly smile. "You're still the true queen, my lady. She's just a shadow in your light."

Gayatri turned, her sari rustling like a warning. "A shadow that steals my place. I won't let her."

Months passed, and whispers spread through Bhaanugarh like wildfire: Geetanjali was pregnant. The kingdom erupted in joy—temple bells rang, their chimes echoing across the hills, and carts laden with sweets rolled through the markets. In the grand dining hall, a feast was held, the tables groaning with platters of saffron rice, spiced lamb, and mango lassis. Inderjeet stood, his royal turban gleaming, his hand clasped around Geetanjali's. Her face glowed, though her eyes held a flicker of nervousness at the court's scrutiny.

"Our child will bring light to Bhaanugarh," Inderjeet declared, his voice ringing with pride. The court clapped, their cheers a wave of sound, but Gayatri sat at the high table, her hands still, her smile a fragile mask. She had no child, no heir, and Geetanjali's joy was a mirror to her own emptiness. Her heart twisted, each clap a reminder of her failure.

That night, Gayatri paced her chambers, her silk sari trailing like a shadow across the marble floor. The moonlight streamed through arched windows, casting her in a ghostly glow. "Why her?" she hissed to Kamla, who stood by the door, her eyes glinting with malice. "Why not me?"

Kamla stepped closer, her voice a venomous whisper. "Patience, my lady. A child is fragile. Accidents happen."

Gayatri froze, her breath catching. The word "accidents" hung in the air, heavy with possibility. She met Kamla's gaze, a silent understanding passing between them. "Yes," Gayatri said slowly, her voice cold. "Accidents."

The day of the birth arrived, the palace alive with anticipation. Geetanjali labored in her chamber, its walls draped with soft blue curtains, the air thick with the scent of medicinal herbs. Midwives bustled, their voices hushed as they tended to her. Outside, Inderjeet paced the corridor, his boots echoing on the stone floor, his heart pounding with hope and fear. "She's strong," he murmured to himself, clutching a prayer bead. "She'll be fine."

Hours dragged, each moment a weight on his chest. Then, a cry pierced the silence—a strong, healthy wail. A midwife emerged, her face beaming. "A boy, Maharaj! A prince!" Inderjeet rushed in, tears brimming as he saw Geetanjali, pale but smiling, cradling a newborn. "Adhirath," he whispered, naming him, his voice thick with emotion. "Our light."

But the midwives whispered among themselves, their eyes wide. "There's another," one said softly. Minutes later, another cry echoed—a girl, delicate but vibrant. Geetanjali, weak but joyful, held her daughter, kissing her tiny forehead. "She's perfect," she whispered, her voice a fragile thread. The girl's smile, small and pure, lit up the dim room like a star.

In the chaos of celebration, Gayatri slipped into the chamber, her movements silent as a shadow. The midwives were distracted, tending to Geetanjali, who lay unconscious, exhausted from the birth. The baby girl slept beside her, wrapped in a soft cotton cloth, her tiny chest rising and falling. Gayatri's heart twisted—she saw Geetanjali's beauty in the child's face, a mirror of her own failure. Her hands trembled as she lifted the baby, her breath shallow. "You won't take my place," she whispered, her voice a venomous hiss.

She stepped into the corridor, where a trusted servant, a gaunt man named Vikram, waited. She pressed a sack of gold coins into his hand, her eyes hard. "Take her to the jungle," she ordered, her voice low. "Leave her there. Tell no one."

Vikram's eyes flickered with fear, but the weight of the coins silenced his doubts. "As you command, my lady," he murmured, taking the baby. He vanished into the night, the child's faint cries fading into the forest's depths.

Hours later, Geetanjali awoke, her eyes searching the bed. "My daughter," she gasped, her voice rising to a scream. "Where is she?" She clutched Inderjeet's arm, her nails digging into his skin. "Inderjeet, where's my princess?"

Inderjeet's face paled, his voice breaking as he shouted, "Search the palace! Find her!" Guards scrambled, their footsteps thundering through the halls. The kingdom turned upside down—servants combed every room, villagers scoured the streets, and priests prayed in the temples. Geetanjali sobbed, her body shaking, her hands clutching the empty cloth where her daughter had lain. "She's gone," she whispered, her voice a wail. "My baby…"

Gayatri stood among the mourners, her face streaked with practiced tears. "Such a tragedy," she said to a courtier, her voice trembling just enough. But inside, her heart was cold, a twisted triumph blooming. She touched her own belly, where her unborn child stirred, a false hope she clung to. "Soon," she murmured to herself, "my child will be the heir."

The palace, once alive with joy, was cloaked in sorrow. The people wept for their Rani of the Heart, their cheers replaced by prayers. Inderjeet stood by Geetanjali's side, his eyes hollow, his hand gripping hers. "We'll find her," he promised, though doubt gnawed at him. "I swear it."

In her chambers, Gayatri sat alone, the moonlight casting her shadow long and dark. Kamla entered, her smile sly. "It's done, my lady. The girl is gone."

Gayatri nodded, but her hands trembled. "Good," she said, her voice hollow. Yet, as she stared into the mirror, she saw not her own face but the baby's smile, haunting her like a ghost. "What have I done?" she whispered, a tear escaping despite her resolve.

The kingdom mourned, its heart broken, but fate was not done with Bhaanugarh. The lost princess, carried away into the jungle, was destined to return, her story a spark that would ignite a saga of love, betrayal, and redemption.

III

A Child of the Jungle

The jungle beyond Bhaanugarh was a realm of shadows and whispers, its dense canopy swallowing the moonlight. Crickets sang a restless chorus, their chirps mingling with the rustle of leaves stirred by a cool night breeze. The air carried the earthy scent of moss and the faint tang of wild berries. Hari and Leela, a farmer couple from Rajgarh, trudged through the trees, their sandals crunching on fallen twigs. Their faces were lined with years of toil, and their hearts bore a quiet ache—they had no children, a void that haunted their simple life. A woven basket of vegetables swung from Hari's shoulder, their meager harvest from a neighbor's field.

Leela's hand tightened on Hari's arm, her steps faltering. "Do you hear that?" she whispered, her voice trembling. A faint cry, fragile as a bird's call, pierced the jungle's hum.

Hari froze, his weathered face tense. "A child?" He squinted into the darkness, the cry growing clearer. "This way," he said, leading Leela toward a small clearing where moonlight spilled through a gap in the trees.

There, on a bed of soft earth, lay a tiny baby wrapped in a tattered cloth. Her face was red from crying, her tiny fists waving in distress. Leela gasped, dropping to her knees beside the child. "Oh, my love," she murmured, lifting the baby into her arms. The infant's cries softened, her wide eyes meeting Leela's. A tentative smile broke through, pure and radiant, like dawn after a storm.

"She's beautiful," Leela whispered, tears streaming down her cheeks. She cradled the baby close, her worn sari brushing the child's delicate skin. "Who could leave you here?"

Hari scanned the clearing, his hand on the hilt of a small knife at his belt. "No one's around," he said, voice low. "This isn't right. Who abandons a child to the jungle?" He knelt beside Leela, his rough fingers brushing the baby's cheek. "She's so small."

"We can't leave her," Leela said, her voice fierce despite her tears. "She's ours now, Hari. The gods sent her to us."

Hari's eyes softened, though worry lingered. "What if someone comes for her? What if—"

"No one's coming," Leela cut in, rocking the baby gently. "Look at her. She needs us." The child cooed, her tiny hand grasping Leela's finger, and Hari's resolve crumbled.

"Alright," he said, his voice thick. "We'll take her home. But we must be careful."

They wrapped the baby in Leela's shawl and hurried to their village in Rajgarh, a cluster of mud huts nestled among golden fields. Their small home was humble, its walls adorned with faded paintings of flowers, its roof thatched with straw. Leela lit a clay lamp, its warm glow dancing across the room. She fed the baby milk from a neighbor's goat, humming a lullaby her mother once sang. "We'll call her Anokhi," she said, smiling at Hari. "Unique, like her spirit."

Hari nodded, watching the baby sleep in Leela's arms. "Anokhi," he repeated, a rare smile breaking through. "Our daughter."

Years passed, and Anokhi grew into a fearless girl, her laughter a melody that echoed through Rajgarh's fields. At sixteen, she was lithe and strong, her dark braid swinging as she hoed the earth beside Hari and Leela. Her hands were calloused from planting rice and harvesting wheat, but her heart was light, filled with love for her parents and the village that embraced her. She raced children through the meadows, shared mangoes with elders, and told stories under the banyan tree, her eyes bright with dreams.

One humid afternoon, Anokhi ventured into the jungle to gather herbs for Leela's fever remedy. The forest was alive with the buzz of cicadas and the scent of damp earth. She hummed softly, her basket half-full, when a guttural roar shattered the calm. Dropping to a crouch, she peered through the undergrowth. There, in a clearing, stood Raja Dev Rana, Rajgarh's aging king, his silver hair disheveled, his royal robe torn. Three wild boars circled him, their tusks gleaming, their snorts loud in the still air. Dev's sword lay just out of reach, knocked away in the struggle.

Anokhi's heart raced, but fear gave way to resolve. She grabbed her bow, a gift from Hari, and nocked an arrow. "Hey!" she shouted, stepping into the clearing. The boars turned, startled, as she fired, the arrow striking the ground near the largest beast. It squealed and retreated, the others following, their hooves thundering into the trees.

Dev staggered, catching his breath, his eyes wide as he looked at his savior. "Who are you, child?" he asked, his voice hoarse but warm.

Anokhi lowered her bow, bowing slightly. "Anokhi, Maharaj. Just a farmer's daughter."

Dev's weathered face broke into a smile, his eyes twinkling. "Just a farmer's daughter? You're a warrior." He retrieved his sword, sheathing it with a shaky hand. "You saved my life. Come to my palace. Let me thank you properly."

Anokhi hesitated, glancing at her basket. "My mother needs these herbs, Maharaj. I must go home."

"Then bring them tomorrow," Dev insisted, his tone kind but firm. "I owe you a debt, Anokhi."

She nodded, a shy smile spreading. "Alright. Tomorrow."

The next day, Anokhi arrived at Dev's palace, a modest fortress of stone and wood, its gates carved with elephants. Dev welcomed her with a feast of rice and curry, his guards watching in awe as the farmer's daughter sat at his table. "You're brave beyond your years," he said, pouring her mango juice. "Where did you learn to shoot like that?"

"My father taught me," Anokhi said, her voice soft with pride. "He says the jungle doesn't care who you are. You must be ready."

Dev chuckled. "Wise words. Stay close, Anokhi. I want to teach you more—swords, horses, the ways of a leader."

Anokhi's eyes widened. "Me? I'm no one special."

"You're wrong," Dev said gently. "You're born to do great things."

From then on, Anokhi became Dev's favorite, like a granddaughter. He trained her in the palace courtyard, her laughter ringing as she parried his strikes or galloped on his finest mare. The villagers whispered of her courage, and Dev's heart swelled with pride. "She's a queen in a farmer's clothes," he told his advisors, his voice firm.

Meanwhile, in Bhaanugarh, sorrow cloaked the palace. Geetanjali, the beloved queen, lay in her chamber, her once-vibrant face pale and hollow. The loss of her daughter had broken her, each day a battle against grief. Inderjeet sat by her bedside, his hand clasping hers, his eyes red from sleepless nights. "Stay with me, my love," he whispered, his voice cracking. "Adhirath needs you. I need you."

Geetanjali's lips trembled, a tear falling. "My daughter," she murmured, her voice barely audible. "Where is she, Inderjeet? I hear her crying..." Her breath faltered, and with a final sigh, she was gone, her last word a whisper: "Anokhi."

Inderjeet buried his face in his hands, his sobs echoing through the marble halls. The kingdom mourned, its flags lowered, its markets silent. Adhirath, now a kind young prince, clung to his father, his heart heavy but his resolve strong. "I'll make you proud, Father," he promised, his voice steady despite his tears.

In her exiled wanderings, Rani Gayatri felt the weight of her sins. Her child, conceived in hope, was born dead, a lifeless bundle that shattered her dreams. She wandered Bhaanugarh's outskirts, her once-regal sari tattered, her beauty faded. At night, she dreamed of a baby's smile, a face that mirrored Geetanjali's. "Anokhi," she whispered in her sleep, waking with a gasp. Guilt gnawed at her, a relentless ghost. "What have I done?" she murmured to the stars, her voice breaking. "Forgive me."

In Rajgarh, Anokhi ran through the fields, unaware of her royal blood. She laughed with Leela, worked beside Hari, and trained with Dev, her spirit a beacon in the humble village. The jungle had given her a new life, but fate was weaving a path back to Bhaanugarh, where her true story waited to unfold.

IV
Shadows of Udaipur

The palace of Udaipur stood proud atop a rugged hill, its sandstone towers piercing a sky streaked with the fiery hues of dusk. Torches blazed along the ramparts, casting a golden glow on the carved arches below, where peacocks strutted in the gardens, their calls mingling with the distant hum of the city. Inside, the air was heavy with the scent of incense and polished wood, but the grandeur masked a colder truth. Raja Dhyan Pratap Singh ruled with a heavy hand, his greed outshining the emerald in his crown. His throne room echoed with demands for taxes, his voice sharp as he dismissed advisors' pleas for mercy. "The kingdom thrives on strength," he barked, his eyes glinting with ambition.

Rani Devi, gentle and soft-spoken, moved through the palace like a quiet breeze, her silk sari shimmering under the chandelier's light. Her love for her sons, Nyay and Vishesh, was her only joy in a court ruled by her husband's iron will. Nyay, now twenty, was tall and handsome, his dark eyes sharp with wisdom, his heart set on justice. He walked the halls with a quiet intensity, greeting servants with a nod, his smile rare but warm. Vishesh, five years younger, was a wiry boy with eager eyes, idolizing Nyay but craving Dhyan's approval, a prize rarely given.

One evening, as the palace glowed under a crescent moon, Nyay slipped through the corridors, his sandals silent on the marble floor. He sought his mother's chambers but paused outside the throne room, where voices drifted through a velvet curtain. Raja Inderjeet Singh, visiting from Bhaanugarh, sat with Dhyan, their goblets clinking with wine. Nyay leaned closer, hidden in the shadows.

"I wanted a daughter," Dhyan sighed, his voice heavy with regret. "Sons bring trouble. A curse lingers over my line, Inderjeet. My father warned me—our blood carries a shadow."

Inderjeet patted his shoulder, his tone warm. "Don't dwell on curses, friend. Your boys are your strength. Nyay's wise beyond his years, and Vishesh has spirit."

Nyay's fists clenched, his heart pounding. A curse? The word struck like a blade, planting a seed of hate. His father's disappointment, so casually spoken, burned in his chest. "I'll never be like him," he vowed under his breath, his voice trembling with resolve. He turned away, the curtain swaying, and fled to the palace gardens, where the cool night air soothed his anger. The stars above seemed to mock him, whispering of a fate he couldn't escape.

The next morning, Udaipur's courtyard rang with the clash of swords. Nyay trained with Adhirath, Bhaanugarh's prince, their blades sparking under the sun. Adhirath, broad-shouldered and kind, dodged Nyay's strike, grinning. "You're too serious, Nyay," he teased, parrying a blow. "Smile sometimes! The world won't end."

Nyay grinned, his tension easing. "And you're too soft, future king. Toughen up!" He lunged, but Adhirath sidestepped, laughing. Their swords clashed again, the rhythm of their sparring a dance of friendship. Servants paused to watch, their cheers a lively hum, and Devi, from a balcony, smiled at her son's rare joy.

"Enough!" Nyay called, lowering his sword, his chest heaving. He clasped Adhirath's shoulder. "You're getting better, but I'm still the champion."

Adhirath laughed, wiping sweat from his brow. "One day, I'll win, and you'll bow to me."

"Dream on," Nyay shot back, their laughter echoing across the courtyard. But beneath his smile, Nyay's heart carried the weight of his father's words, a shadow that lingered even in the sunlight.

That evening, Nyay rode to Rajgarh to seek Raja Dev Rana, whose wisdom was a balm to his restless soul. Dev's palace, smaller but warm, welcomed him with open gates. They sat by a fountain, its water sparkling under lantern light. "You look troubled, boy," Dev said, his silver hair glinting, his eyes kind but sharp.

Nyay hesitated, then spoke. "My father... he spoke of a curse. He's ashamed of me, of Vishesh. I don't want to be like him, Maharaj."

Dev's hand rested on Nyay's shoulder. "You're not him, Nyay. You've got a heart that seeks justice, not gold. That's your strength."

Nyay's throat tightened. "But what if the curse is real? What if I fail?"

"Then you fight it," Dev said firmly. "A true leader shapes his own fate."

Their talk was interrupted by a festival in Rajgarh's market, where drums thundered and lanterns floated like fireflies. Nyay and Adhirath, who had joined them, competed in a horse race, their stallions galloping through cheering crowds. Dust swirled, and the air rang with shouts as Nyay's horse surged ahead, crossing the finish line first. The crowd roared, and Dev clapped, his voice booming. "You're a born leader, Nyay!"

Nyay dismounted, his heart light, but Vishesh's absence gnawed at him. His brother had stayed behind, trailing Dhyan like a shadow, desperate for a nod of approval. At dinner, Devi noticed Nyay's quiet mood. "Where's Vishesh?" she asked, her voice soft.

"Pleasing Father," Nyay said, his tone bitter. "He thinks it'll earn him love."

Devi's eyes saddened. "He's young, Nyay. He looks up to you, too."

Nyay nodded, but doubt lingered. "I'll try, Mother. For you."

Meanwhile, in Bhaanugarh, the palace was a quieter place, its halls heavy with Geetanjali's absence. Rani Gayatri, exiled but lingering in the city's shadows, sought to fill the void of her stillborn child. She adopted a girl, Tejaswi, from a troupe of performers, hoping to mend her broken heart. Tejaswi, sharp-tongued and ambitious, stood in the palace courtyard, her dark eyes scanning the opulent surroundings. Adhirath, now a kind young prince, approached, holding a silver bangle. "For you, Tejaswi," he said, smiling. "Welcome to our family."

Tejaswi's lips curled into a sneer. "You're no brother of mine," she snapped, storming off, the bangle untouched. Her heart burned with dreams of a crown, not sibling bonds.

Adhirath sighed, watching her go. "She's family, whether she likes it or not," he murmured to a guard, his voice heavy with resolve. He turned to the horizon, where Udaipur's hills loomed, unaware of the storm brewing there.

Back in Udaipur, Vishesh lingered outside Dhyan's chambers, clutching a polished dagger he'd crafted as a gift. "Father," he called, his voice eager. "I made this for you."

Dhyan barely glanced at it, waving him away. "Put it with the others, boy. I'm busy." Vishesh's face fell, his hands trembling as he retreated. In the corridor, he passed Nyay, who paused, seeing his brother's pain.

"Vishesh," Nyay said softly, "come train with me tomorrow. We'll show Father what we're made of."

Vishesh's eyes brightened, but his voice was small. "He doesn't care, Bhaiya. Not about me."

Nyay knelt, gripping his brother's shoulders. "I care. You're my brother. That's enough."

Vishesh nodded, a faint smile breaking through, but the seed of his father's neglect took root, a quiet ache that would grow. Nyay watched him go, his heart heavy. He thought of Dev's words—shape your own fate—but the curse Dhyan spoke of loomed like a shadow over his family.

As the festival lights faded, Udaipur's palace stood silent, its towers stark against the starry sky. Nyay lay awake, his mind racing with his father's words, his brother's pain, and his own vow to be different. In Bhaanugarh, Tejaswi plotted, her eyes on a throne she'd never share. The kingdoms were bound by friendship and blood, but beneath the surface, cracks were forming—cracks that would lead to betrayal, war, and a destiny none could foresee.

V

A Fateful Encounter

The Rajgarh jungle was a labyrinth of green, its towering trees woven with vines that draped like curtains. The air was thick with the scent of moss and damp earth, pierced by the sharp tang of wildflowers. Sunlight filtered through the canopy, casting dappled patterns on the forest floor, where the buzz of cicadas and the distant call of a hornbill created a living symphony. Nyay Pratap Singh, prince of Udaipur, guided his black stallion through the narrow paths, his royal kurta clinging to his skin in the humid heat. He rode to Raja Dev Rana's palace, seeking the old king's wisdom to ease the weight of his father's words—a curse that haunted his thoughts. But upon arriving, a guard informed him Dev was away, visiting distant villages.

Nyay's eyes wandered to the jungle's depths, where whispers spoke of a wish-granting tree, a sacred place where dreams were said to take root. Curiosity tugged at him, a rare lightness in his heart. "I'll find it," he murmured, dismounting and tethering his horse. In a reckless moment, he left his sword strapped to the saddle—a mistake that would nearly cost him his life.

The path grew wilder, roots snaking across the earth like veins. Nyay pushed through, his boots sinking into soft mud, until he reached a clearing. There stood the tree, ancient and gnarled, its branches heavy with colorful threads tied by hopeful souls. He touched the bark, his fingers tracing its rough surface. "If you're real," he whispered, "grant me a heart free of my father's shadow." The words felt fragile, a plea he barely dared voice.

A low growl shattered the silence. Nyay froze, his breath catching. From the shadows, a pride of lions emerged, their amber eyes locked on him, their tawny fur rippling with muscle. Their growls shook the air, a primal warning that sent his heart pounding. He backed against the tree, his hands empty, his sword a distant regret. "Stay calm," he muttered, but panic clawed at his chest. The lead lion crouched, its tail flicking, ready to lunge.

A sharp whistle sliced through the air, followed by the twang of a bowstring. An arrow struck the ground near the lion's paw, kicking up dirt. The beast roared, startled, and the others hesitated. Hooves thundered, and a girl on a black mare burst into the clearing, her bow drawn, another arrow nocked. Her dark braid whipped behind her, her eyes fierce as a storm. "Move!" she shouted, firing again, the arrow grazing the lion's flank. The pride scattered, their roars fading into the jungle.

Nyay stumbled forward, his legs weak, as the girl reined in her horse. She was Anokhi, her mud-streaked lehenga clinging to her frame, her face flushed with adrenaline. Her bow remained steady, her gaze scanning the trees for lingering threats. "You alright?" she asked, her voice sharp but laced with concern.

Nyay nodded, catching his breath. "You saved my life," he said, his voice hoarse. "I'm Nyay."

She lowered her bow, studying him with a smirk. "Anokhi. Next time, bring a sword, Palace boy." Her tone was teasing, but her eyes held a spark of curiosity.

He laughed, a nervous sound that broke the tension. "You're not like anyone I've met."

"And you're not like most fools who wander into lion dens," she shot back, dismounting with a grace that belied her farmer's attire. She tethered her horse, then gestured to him. "Come on, I'll get you out of here before you tempt fate again."

Nyay hesitated, then climbed onto her horse behind her. As they galloped through the jungle, the wind roared in his ears, carrying the scent of her—earth and jasmine. His hands rested lightly on her waist, and a strange warmth bloomed in his chest. "You're good with that bow," he said, raising his voice over the hoofbeats.

"Had to be," she replied, her tone matter-of-fact. "The jungle doesn't wait for you to learn."

They reached the edge of her family's fields, where golden wheat swayed under a fading sun. Anokhi dismounted, tying her horse to a tamarind tree. Nyay followed, his royal boots sinking into the soft soil. The fields stretched wide, framed by distant hills, and the air was alive with the chirp of sparrows settling for the night. "This is my home," Anokhi said, her voice softening. "You can walk to the village from here."

Nyay's gaze lingered on her, her fierce spirit tempered by a quiet pride. "Why did you save me?" he asked, stepping closer. "You didn't know me."

Anokhi shrugged, but her eyes met his, unguarded. "No one deserves to die like that. Besides, you looked too scared to leave behind." She grinned, and Nyay couldn't help but smile back.

Their moment was broken by a deep chuckle. Raja Dev Rana strode toward them, his silver hair glinting in the twilight, his royal robe dusty from travel. "Anokhi, my brave girl!" he called, his eyes twinkling. "Nyay, you're lucky she was here."

Anokhi rolled her eyes, crossing her arms. "Dada Maharaj, he's trouble. I've got work to do." She turned to the fields, her braid swaying, but Nyay's gaze followed her, a pull he couldn't name.

Dev nudged him, his voice low. "She's special, Nyay. Like a granddaughter to me. Want me to talk to your father?" He winked, his grin mischievous.

Nyay flushed, his heart racing. "I just met her, Maharaj! Give me a chance to breathe."

Dev laughed, clapping his shoulder. "Take your time, boy. But don't wait too long."

As Nyay rode back to Udaipur, Anokhi's courage lingered in his mind, a light against the shadow of his father's curse. Days later, he returned to Rajgarh, his royal attire traded for a simple kurta, his heart drawn to her fields. He found Anokhi and her father, Hari, planting rice under a scorching sun. "I need a job," Nyay said, grinning, though his palms sweated with nerves.

Hari, a wiry man with kind eyes, hesitated. "We barely earn enough for ourselves, lad. Times are hard."

"One meal a day," Nyay offered, his voice earnest. "I'll work hard, I swear."

Anokhi raised an eyebrow, her hands on her hips. "You? A Palace boy, farming? This I've got to see."

Hari sighed, glancing at Anokhi. "Alright, but you pull your weight."

Nyay nodded, rolling up his sleeves. He toiled beside Anokhi, his hands blistered by the hoe, his back aching under the sun's glare. She teased him mercilessly, laughing when he stumbled in the mud. "Not so princely now, are you?" she said, tossing him a water gourd.

He drank deeply, grinning. "I'm learning, farmer girl. Give me time."

At dusk, they sat under a banyan tree, sharing a simple meal of roti and lentil stew, the stars emerging above. Leela, Anokhi's mother, joined them, her smile warm. "You're a quick learner, Nyay," she said, passing him a mango. "But why leave your city for this?"

Nyay's smile faded, his voice soft. "My home's heavy with rules and shadows. Here, I feel... free."

Anokhi's eyes met his, a quiet understanding passing between them. "Freedom's hard-won," she said, her tone gentle. "But it's worth it."

Hari watched them, his gaze thoughtful. "You're welcome here, Nyay. But don't break her heart."

Nyay's cheeks burned, but he nodded. "I won't, Mr.Farmer. I promise."

As the fireflies danced, Nyay felt a peace he'd never known, a moment of light in a life shadowed by duty. Anokhi's laughter, her fierce spirit, stirred his heart, a spark that would grow into a flame. In Udaipur, his father's curse waited, but here, under Rajgarh's stars, Nyay dared to dream of a future shaped by love, not fate.

VI

A Kingdom's Sorrow

Bhaanugarh's palace, once a beacon of light, was draped in mourning, its marble walls dulled by grief. Black banners hung from the towers, swaying in the cool night breeze, their edges frayed like the kingdom's heart. The scent of sandalwood lingered from funeral pyres, and the distant wail of a flute carried Geetanjali's absence through the halls. Raja Inderjeet Singh stood in the royal courtyard, his eyes hollow, his once-regal frame stooped under the weight of loss. Geetanjali's death had carved a void in his soul, her final whisper—"Anokhi"—a wound that refused to heal. Adhirath, now a young man of twenty, ruled with kindness, his gentle voice soothing the court, but even his warmth couldn't fill the silence left by his mother.

In the shadows of the palace, Rani Gayatri's secret festered, a poison that haunted her dreams. Her chambers, stripped of their former splendor, felt like a cage. She sat before a cracked mirror, her silk sari tattered, her face gaunt from sleepless nights. The baby's smile—Geetanjali's daughter—flashed in her mind, a ghost of her crime. Her maid, Kamla, had grown bold, her loyalty wavering as whispers of reward reached her ears. One evening, Kamla slipped into the throne room, where Inderjeet sat alone, his crown discarded on the table.

"My lord," Kamla said, her voice low, "I know the truth about your daughter. Gayatri took her. She paid a servant to leave her in the jungle."

Inderjeet's head snapped up, his eyes blazing. "Speak plainly, woman!" he roared, rising. "What did she do?"

Kamla trembled but held her ground, her greed outweighing fear. "She stole the princess, Maharaj. Out of envy. I saw her give the gold, heard her orders."

The court was summoned, the air thick with tension as Gayatri was dragged before Inderjeet. Her hair was disheveled, her eyes wild with defiance and dread. The nobles whispered, their faces a mix of shock and pity. Adhirath stood beside his father, his heart torn between justice and sorrow. "Is it true?" Inderjeet asked, his voice trembling, a father's pain breaking through his kingly mask. "Did you take my daughter?"

Gayatri's lips quivered, her gaze darting to Kamla, who smirked from the shadows. "I... I was protecting my place," she stammered, her voice cracking. "Geetanjali took everything—your love, the throne. I had to act!"

Inderjeet's face crumpled, his hands shaking. "You took my daughter," he said, each word a dagger. "You broke Geetanjali's heart. Leave, Gayatri. Never return." His voice broke, and he turned away, unable to bear her sight.

Gayatri fell to her knees, her sobs echoing in the silent hall. "Inderjeet, please," she begged, reaching for him. "I was wrong, but I loved you!" Guards seized her, dragging her out as she wailed, her cries fading into the night. She wandered Bhaanugarh's streets, her riches gone, her guilt a heavy cloak. At a roadside shrine, she knelt, tears falling. "Forgive me, child," she whispered to the stars, her voice raw. "I didn't know the cost."

In Bhaanugarh's palace, Adhirath faced Tejaswi, the adopted girl Gayatri had raised. Now a young woman, Tejaswi's sharp features hid a burning ambition. She stood in the garden, her silk lehenga catching the moonlight, her eyes cold as she watched Adhirath approach. "You're king now," she said, her voice edged with scorn. "But I'm no sister to you."

Adhirath's smile was patient,

In Rajgarh, Anokhi's world shattered under a merciless sun. Her father, Hari, lay in their mud hut, his breathing ragged from a fever that refused to break. Leela, her mother, knelt beside him, her hands trembling as she pressed a damp cloth to his forehead. Anokhi, now sixteen, stood frozen, her heart pounding. "He'll be fine, Ma," she said, her voice shaking. "He's strong."

Leela's eyes were red, her voice soft. "Pray, Anokhi. Pray hard."

That night, Hari's breath stopped, his hand slipping from Leela's grasp. Anokhi knelt by his body, her sobs tearing through the quiet hut. "Papa," she wailed, clutching his still hand. "Don't leave me. You're my everything." The clay lamp flickered, casting her grief in trembling shadows.

Word reached Nyay in Udaipur, and he rode to Rajgarh, his heart heavy. He found Anokhi by the fields, her face streaked with tears, her lehenga dusty from kneeling. "Anokhi," he said, dismounting, his voice gentle. He pulled her into his arms, her sobs muffled against his chest. "I can't feel your pain, but I'm here."

She leaned into him, her tears falling. "He was my strength, Nyay. What do I do now?"

He guided her to sit under a tamarind tree, the moon casting a silver glow over the fields. Crickets sang softly, a quiet comfort. "You're strong, Anokhi," Nyay said, his voice steady. "Stronger than me. He'd be proud."

Anokhi wiped her eyes, a faint smile breaking through. "You're not so bad, city boy," she whispered, her voice raw but warm.

Nyay shared stories of his childhood—stealing mangoes with Vishesh, hiding from their tutor. Anokhi laughed softly, her grief easing. "You were a troublemaker," she teased, nudging him.

"Still am," he said, grinning, but his eyes held a tenderness that warmed her heart. They sat in silence, the stars above them a canvas of hope, their bond growing like the roots of the tree.

In Udaipur, tension brewed in the palace's golden halls. Raja Dhyan announced at a grand feast, his voice booming, "I'll name my successor soon. Udaipur needs a strong king." The court buzzed, nobles exchanging glances. Vishesh, eager to please, hovered near Dhyan, his eyes bright with hope. "I'll make you proud, Father," he said, offering a polished goblet.

Dhyan nodded absently, his attention on advisors. "Good, boy. Stay sharp." Vishesh's smile faltered, his heart aching for more. He grew distant from Nyay, who spent more time in Rajgarh, drawn to Anokhi's light.

Tejaswi visited Udaipur, her ambition trailing her like a shadow. She found Nyay in the palace garden, practicing archery. "I'll cook for you," she offered, her voice sweet, her eyes calculating. "A prince deserves a good meal."

Nyay smiled, but his thoughts were with Anokhi. "Cook yourself, Tejaswi. Anokhi taught me—hard work matters."

Tejaswi's smile faded, her fingers tightening on her shawl. "A farmer's daughter? She's nothing."

Nyay's jaw tightened, his voice cold. "She's everything." He walked away, leaving Tejaswi seething, her heart burning with jealousy. "I'll show him," she muttered, her eyes narrowing. "I'll be his queen."

That night, Nyay lay awake in Udaipur, Anokhi's tear-streaked face haunting him. He thought of her strength, her laughter, and felt a pull he couldn't name. In Rajgarh, Anokhi sat by Hari's grave, Leela's hand on her shoulder. "He's watching you, beta," Leela said, her voice soft. "Live bravely, for him."

Anokhi nodded, her heart heavy but resolute. "I will, Ma." She looked to the stars, unaware that her courage would soon draw her into a storm of royal intrigue, where love and betrayal waited.

In Bhaanugarh, Adhirath stood on the palace balcony, the city's lights twinkling below. "Mother, I'll find her," he whispered, his voice a vow to Geetanjali's memory. The kingdoms of Bhaanugarh, Udaipur, and Rajgarh were bound by grief and ambition, their fates converging on a path where Anokhi's light would either heal or burn.

his heart heavy. "Tejaswi, we're family. Let me help you."

She laughed, bitter. "Family? I'll be queen one day, Adhirath. Not your shadow." She stormed off, her heart twisted by dreams of power.

Tejaswi's gaze often lingered on Nyay, Udaipur's prince, who visited Bhaanugarh frequently. His laughter with Adhirath, their easy bond, sparked envy in her chest. "I'll be queen," she vowed, her voice a whisper in her chamber, her fingers clutching a silver comb Nyay had once admired.

VII
A Murder's Shadow

Udaipur's palace glowed under a starlit sky, its sandstone towers adorned with crimson and gold banners that fluttered in the warm night breeze. The courtyard buzzed with festivity, lanterns casting a golden haze over tables laden with saffron rice, roasted meats, and mango sweets. Drummers pounded rhythms that pulsed through the air, and dancers in swirling lehengas spun like flames, their anklets jingling. The kingdom had gathered to hear Raja Dhyan Pratap Singh announce his successor, a moment that would shape Udaipur's future. Yet beneath the joy, tension crackled like a storm waiting to break.

Nyay and Vishesh stood side by side near the throne, their royal kurtas gleaming with silver embroidery. Nyay, tall and composed, scanned the crowd, his dark eyes heavy with unease. Vishesh, younger and restless, fidgeted, his gaze darting to their father's empty throne. The brothers' bond, once unbreakable, strained under the weight of Dhyan's looming decision. "You're quiet, Bhaiya," Vishesh said, his voice low, a forced smile on his lips. "Nervous?"

Nyay's jaw tightened, his thoughts on Anokhi's fields, a world away from this glittering cage. "Just thinking," he replied, his tone clipped. "Father's choice changes everything."

Vishesh's smile faded, his eyes narrowing. "He'll pick you. He always does." The words carried a sting, a jealousy Vishesh couldn't hide.

Before Nyay could respond, trumpets blared, and Dhyan entered, his crown glinting, his stride commanding. Rani Devi followed, her gentle face strained, her hands clasped tightly. The crowd hushed as Dhyan raised a hand. "Tonight, Udaipur looks to the future," he boomed. "My successor will lead with strength. Tomorrow, I name him."

The court erupted in cheers, but Nyay's heart sank, sensing the shadow of his father's curse. That night, the palace grew quiet, the revelry fading into whispers. Nyay wandered the corridors, unable to sleep, when a scream shattered the silence. Guards rushed toward Dhyan's chambers, their torches casting frantic shadows. Nyay followed, dread pooling in his chest.

Inside, Dhyan lay sprawled on his silken bed, a dagger buried in his chest, his eyes staring blankly at the ceiling. Blood stained the sheets, a crimson pool spreading like a curse fulfilled. Beside him lay a dagger with Nyay's crest, its blade glinting cruelly in the lamplight. A guard, his face pale, pointed at Nyay. "I saw him near the chambers, his cloak bloodied!" he stammered, his voice shaking.

Nyay's world tilted. "That's a lie!" he shouted, stepping back as guards seized his arms. "I was in the gardens! I didn't do this!"

Chaos erupted. Devi collapsed, her sobs tearing through the room as she clutched Dhyan's lifeless hand. "My love," she wailed, her voice breaking. "Who did this to you?"

Vishesh stood frozen, tears streaming down his face, his eyes locking onto Nyay with a mix of grief and accusation. "You hated Father!" he cried, his voice raw. "You wanted the throne!"

Nyay struggled against the guards, his heart pounding. "Vishesh, no! I'd never hurt him! You know me!"

But the crowd's boos drowned him out, their faces twisted with anger. Tejaswi, who had arrived from Bhaanugarh, stepped forward, her silk sari shimmering, her voice cold as ice. "Maybe Nyay knew Father chose Vishesh," she said, her eyes glinting with malice. "He couldn't bear it."

Devi's head snapped up, her voice trembling. "Tejaswi, hold your tongue! Nyay's my son!"

Tejaswi's lips curved, but she said no more, her words a poison already spread. The court, swayed by grief and fear, sentenced Nyay to life in prison. He was dragged to the dungeons, his hands bound, his shouts echoing. "I'm innocent!" he roared, but the iron bars clanged shut, sealing his fate.

In Rajgarh, dawn painted the fields golden, but Anokhi's heart was heavy as she worked beside Leela. Raja Dev Rana sat under a banyan tree, his face grim as he shared the news from Udaipur. "Nyay's accused of killing Dhyan," he said, his voice low. "They found his dagger, a guard saw him."

Anokhi's hoe fell, her eyes blazing. "He's no killer," she said, her voice firm. "Nyay hates violence. He'd die before hurting his father."

Dev sighed, his silver hair catching the light. "The evidence is strong, Anokhi. And Dhyan's curse... maybe it's true."

She shook her head, her necklace—a gift from Leela—glinting at her throat. "Curses don't make men murderers. Someone's lying." She turned to Leela, her voice urgent. "Ma, I'm going to him. He needs me."

Leela's eyes softened, but worry creased her face. "Be careful, beta. Royals play dangerous games."

Anokhi rode to Udaipur, her horse kicking up dust, her heart a drumbeat of resolve. The dungeon was a maze of damp stone, its air cold and sour. Nyay sat in a cell, his face pale, his kurta torn. His eyes lit up when he saw her, a spark of hope in the gloom. "Anokhi," he whispered, gripping the bars. "I didn't do it. Someone's framing me."

She clutched the bars, her knuckles white, her voice fierce. "I believe you, Nyay. I'll find the truth, I swear."

He reached through, his fingers brushing hers. "You're my light," he said, his voice cracking. "Talk to Adhirath in Bhaanugarh. He'll help."

Anokhi nodded, tears burning her eyes. "Stay strong, city boy. I'm not losing you." She turned away, her heart heavy but her resolve iron.

In Bhaanugarh, the palace stood solemn, its marble halls echoing with Adhirath's quiet rule. Anokhi stormed in, her farmer's lehenga out of place among the silks, her necklace glinting—a twin to one Adhirath wore, though neither knew it. She found him in the throne room, his face weary. "You know Nyay's innocent," she said, her voice sharp. "Why didn't you speak for him?"

Adhirath sent the guards away, his eyes searching hers. "The evidence was too strong, Anokhi. The dagger, the guard's word—I couldn't sway the court."

Her eyes flashed, her hands fisted. "Then you're no friend. He's rotting in a cell, and you sit here playing king!"

Adhirath flinched, his voice low. "I'm trying to help him, quietly. Accusing the court would've made it worse."

Anokhi stepped closer, her voice trembling. "Then come with me to Rajgarh. Dev will know what to do. Nyay trusts you—don't fail him."

Adhirath hesitated, then nodded, his jaw set. "For Nyay," he said, his eyes catching her necklace, a flicker of curiosity passing unnoticed.

That night, in Udaipur, Vishesh sat alone in Dhyan's chambers, clutching the dagger he'd crafted for his father, now stained with blood. "Why, Bhaiya?" he whispered, tears falling. "Why take him from me?" His heart twisted with grief and betrayal, unaware of the truth hidden in Tejaswi's sly smiles.

Tejaswi, in her guest chamber, penned a letter, her quill scratching furiously. "Nyay's gone," she murmured, her voice cold. "Now Vishesh will be king—and I'll be his queen." She sealed the letter, her ambition a flame that burned brighter than her conscience.

In Rajgarh, Anokhi and Adhirath prepared to meet Dev, their horses tethered under a starry sky. Anokhi touched her necklace, her heart heavy with Nyay's pale face. "We'll save him," she told Adhirath, her voice fierce. "No matter what."

Adhirath nodded, his own necklace glinting, a clue to a truth yet to unfold. "For Nyay," he said, his voice a vow.

The palace of Udaipur, once festive, now stood silent, its banners drooping like broken promises. Nyay's cell was cold, but Anokhi's faith warmed him, a spark in the darkness. In Bhaanugarh, the necklace's secret waited, a thread tying Anokhi to her lost family. The kingdoms were bound by blood and betrayal, their fates converging on a truth that would either free Nyay or destroy them all.

VIII
The Twin's Truth

The Rajgarh jungle shimmered under a late afternoon sun, its dense canopy filtering golden light onto the mossy earth below. The air was thick with the scent of wild jasmine and the hum of unseen creatures, a living tapestry that cloaked the modest stone palace of Raja Dev Rana. Inside, the air was cooler, the walls adorned with faded tapestries of warriors and elephants. Anokhi and Adhirath sat across from Dev in his private chamber, a low wooden table between them strewn with maps and scrolls. Anokhi's heart raced, her fingers fidgeting with the silver necklace Leela had given her, its pendant a delicate lotus etched with tiny vines.

Dev leaned forward, his silver hair catching the lamplight, his weathered hands gently lifting Anokhi's necklace. His eyes widened, a gasp escaping his lips. "This belonged to Geetanjali," he said, his voice trembling with awe. "I saw her wear it on her wedding day. Anokhi, you're her daughter—Bhaanugarh's lost princess."

Anokhi's breath caught, her world tilting. "That's impossible," she whispered, her voice shaking. "I'm a farmer's daughter. Leela and Hari raised me."

Adhirath, seated beside her, stared at his own necklace, identical to hers, its lotus pendant glinting in his hand. His face paled, his eyes locking onto Anokhi's. "You're my sister," he whispered, his voice thick with emotion. He stood, pulling her into a fierce hug, his arms trembling. "I've dreamed of you my whole life."

Anokhi stiffened, her heart torn between joy and shock. She pushed back gently, her eyes glistening. "Adhirath, we focus on Nyay first," she said, her voice firm but cracking. "He's in danger. Then we tell the world."

Adhirath nodded, wiping his eyes, his smile both proud and pained. "You're as strong as Mother was," he said softly. "Let's save him."

Dev cleared his throat, his gaze steady. "The dagger in Dhyan's chamber—it's the key. If it's a forgery, it proves Nyay's innocence."

Anokhi's mind sharpened, her farmer's eye for detail stirring. They traveled to Udaipur's market, where a blacksmith examined the dagger's crest under a flickering torch. "It's a fake," he muttered, pointing to a subtle flaw in the etching—a line too shallow, a curve misaligned. "Nyay's crest is finer work."

Anokhi's heart leaped. "Who could forge it?" she asked, her voice urgent.

The blacksmith hesitated, then whispered, "Ask the guard who saw Nyay that night. He's been spending gold beyond his means."

Anokhi tracked the guard to a tavern, its air thick with smoke and laughter. She cornered him in a shadowy alcove, her bow slung across her back, her eyes fierce. "You lied about Nyay," she said, her voice low. "Who paid you?"

The guard's face paled, his hands trembling. "Tejaswi," he stammered. "She gave me gold to say I saw him, to plant the dagger. I didn't know they'd kill the king!"

Anokhi's fists clenched, her heart pounding. "You'll tell the court," she ordered, her voice steel. "Or I'll drag you there myself."

Meanwhile, in Udaipur's dungeon, Nyay seized a moment of chaos—a guard's dropped keys during a meal delivery. He slipped from his cell, his heart racing, and fled into Rajgarh's jungle, his torn kurta snagging on thorns. Exhausted, he collapsed by a stream, its water cold against his fevered skin. Anokhi found him at dawn, guided by tracks only her jungle-trained eyes could read. "Nyay!" she cried, dropping to her knees beside him.

He pulled her close, his arms weak but desperate. "You're my strength," he whispered, his voice hoarse, his eyes shining with relief.

Anokhi smiled, tears falling. "And you're mine, prince or not." She bandaged his cuts with strips of her dupatta, her hands steady despite her trembling heart. "We know the truth now. Tejaswi framed you."

Nyay's eyes darkened. "Why? What does she gain?"

Before she could answer, Dev approached, his horse tethered nearby. He sat with them, his face grim. "Dhyan's past holds the answer," he said, his voice heavy. "He killed my family to seize Rajgarh's throne, long ago. A priest cursed him—his sons would die fighting. Nyay, your hatred for him makes sense now, but you must break that curse."

Nyay's jaw tightened, his voice raw. "I hated him, but I didn't kill him. I'll prove it, for Vishesh, for Mother."

Anokhi squeezed his hand. "We'll do it together."

In Udaipur, the palace's golden halls hid darker schemes. Tejaswi stood in Vishesh's chambers, her silk sari shimmering, her eyes cold. "Anokhi's a threat," she said, her voice a venomous whisper. "She's the real princess of Bhaanugarh. If she lives, she'll claim everything—Nyay, the throne."

Vishesh's face hardened, his grief for Dhyan twisting into rage. "And Nyay," he said, his voice dark. "Father chose him. I was never enough."

Tejaswi's hand rested on his arm, her smile sly. "We'll rule together, Vishesh. But they must be gone."

He nodded, his eyes distant. "For Father," he murmured, clutching the dagger he'd once crafted, its blade now a symbol of his pain.

Anokhi, traveling to Udaipur for evidence, paused at a roadside shrine where Gayatri, now a wanderer, knelt in tattered robes. Overhearing Gayatri's confession to Tejaswi, who had sought her out, Anokhi's blood ran cold. "I took Geetanjali's daughter," Gayatri wept, her voice breaking. "I left her in the jungle, out of envy. I destroyed everything."

Tejaswi's eyes narrowed. "Keep quiet, old woman. That girl's a ghost now."

Anokhi stepped forward, her heart pounding, her necklace glinting. "No, I'm alive," she said, her voice trembling with rage and pain. "You stole my life, Gayatri."

Gayatri fell to her knees, her face crumpling. "Forgive me," she sobbed, reaching for Anokhi's hem. "I was blind with envy. I see your mother in you, and it breaks me."

Anokhi's eyes burned, her heart torn between fury and pity. "I can't forgive you yet," she said, her voice cracking. "But I won't let your hate destroy me." She turned away, her focus on Nyay, her resolve a flame against the darkness.

That night, in Rajgarh's fields, Anokhi and Nyay sat under a starry sky, Adhirath and Dev nearby, planning their next move. "The guard will confess," Anokhi said, her voice steady. "We'll clear your name."

Nyay took her hand, his eyes soft. "You've given me hope, Anokhi. Whatever happens, I'm yours."

She smiled, her heart swelling. "And I'm yours, city boy. No throne can change that."

Adhirath watched them, his own necklace heavy with meaning. "You're my sister," he said, his voice warm. "But you're also a queen, Anokhi. Don't forget it."

Dev nodded, his eyes proud. "Geetanjali's spirit lives in you. Lead with her heart."

In Udaipur, Vishesh stood on the palace balcony, the city's lights twinkling below. Tejaswi joined him, her voice soft but sharp. "We act soon," she said. "Before they ruin us."

Vishesh's grip tightened on the railing, his heart heavy. "For Father," he whispered, unaware of the truth that would shatter his world.

Anokhi returned to Rajgarh, her mind racing with Gayatri's confession, the guard's betrayal, and Nyay's freedom. She touched her necklace, now a symbol of her lost family, and vowed to reclaim her place—not for revenge, but for justice. The jungle whispered around her, its secrets entwined with her destiny, a path that would lead to war, love, and a truth that could heal or destroy.

In Bhaanugarh, Adhirath prepared to rally Nyay's supporters, his heart full of hope for his newfound sister. The kingdoms of Udaipur, Rajgarh, and Bhaanugarh stood on the edge of chaos, their fates bound by a princess who was born to rule.

IX

The War of Brothers

Udaipur's once-glorious palace stood battered under a sky heavy with storm clouds, its golden towers dulled by the chaos that gripped the city. The streets echoed with the cries of merchants closing shops and mothers calling children indoors, as Vishesh, now king, ruled with an iron fist. His decrees—heavy taxes, curfews, and conscriptions—squeezed the life from Udaipur's people, their faces gaunt with fear and hunger. Tejaswi, his new queen, stood beside him, her silk sari shimmering in the throne room, her eyes gleaming with ambition. "Bhaanugarh's throne will be ours," she whispered to Vishesh, her voice a venomous promise. "Anokhi's claim means nothing."

In Rajgarh's lush fields, Anokhi and Adhirath rallied Nyay's supporters—farmers, merchants, and exiled nobles who believed in his innocence. Under the shade of a tamarind tree, Anokhi addressed the crowd, her lehenga dusty but her voice steady. "Nyay's no murderer," she declared, her bow slung across her back. "Vishesh and Tejaswi framed him. We fight for justice, for Udaipur's heart!"

The crowd roared, their fists raised, but Adhirath's hand on her shoulder steadied her. "You're their princess," he said softly, his necklace glinting, a twin to hers. "They'll follow you to the end."

Anokhi's eyes softened, but her resolve hardened. "Then let's bring Nyay home."

The night before the battle, Nyay met Anokhi by Rajgarh's river, its waters shimmering under a crescent moon. The air was cool, carrying the scent of wet earth and jasmine. Nyay's armor lay nearby, his kurta loose, his face etched with determination. He took her hands, his fingers warm against her calloused palms. "I love you, Anokhi," he said, his voice steady but thick with emotion. "If I live, I'll marry you and make you Udaipur's queen."

Anokhi's eyes shone with tears, her heart swelling. "Come back to me, Nyay," she whispered, her voice trembling. She leaned into him, their foreheads touching, the river's soft lapping their only witness.

He kissed her gently, a promise sealed in the quiet night. "I will," he said, his voice a vow. "No curse can stop me."

Dawn broke over Udaipur's fields, the sky a tumult of black clouds and lightning. The battle raged, a symphony of chaos—swords clashed, arrows whistled, and war cries echoed across the muddy plains. Nyay led his forces, his blade flashing as he cut through Vishesh's guards, his heart heavy with the fight against his brother. Anokhi, atop a hill, wielded her bow with deadly precision, her arrows protecting Nyay from flanking soldiers. Adhirath fought beside her, his sword a blur, their bond unspoken but fierce.

"Stay sharp, sister!" he shouted, parrying a blow.

Anokhi grinned, nocking another arrow. "You too, brother!" she called, her heart swelling with pride.

In the heart of the battlefield, Nyay faced Vishesh, their blades sparking under the stormy sky. Vishesh's crown was crooked, his eyes wild with rage and grief. "Why, brother?" Nyay shouted, dodging a strike. "Why kill Father? We could've been a family!"

Vishesh sneered, his voice bitter. "He chose you! I was nothing to him. I had to act!" His sword swung, but Nyay parried, their clash a dance of betrayal.

"You're wrong!" Nyay cried, his voice breaking. "He loved you, Vishesh. Tejaswi poisoned you!"

Vishesh faltered, doubt flickering in his eyes, but his blade rose again. "Lies!" he roared, lunging. Nyay sidestepped, his sword striking true, piercing Vishesh's chest. The young king fell, blood staining the earth, his last words a whisper: "The curse..." His eyes closed, his crown rolling into the mud.

Nyay dropped to his knees, tears mixing with rain. "I'm sorry, brother," he sobbed, clutching Vishesh's hand. "I failed you."

Anokhi rushed to him, her bow discarded, her arms pulling him close. "You fought for truth," she whispered, her voice steady despite her tears. "He's at peace now."

Tejaswi, seeing Vishesh fall, fled the battlefield, her sari torn, her dreams crumbling. Adhirath's men captured her in a nearby village, her face streaked with dirt and defiance. A search of her chambers uncovered letters to Vishesh, their ink damning—plots to kill Anokhi, to frame Nyay, to seize Bhaanugarh's throne. In Udaipur's court, now somber and scarred, Tejaswi stood trial. "I did it for love," she spat, her eyes cold. "Vishesh deserved to be king."

Devi, seated beside the throne, stood, her voice trembling but firm. "You destroyed my sons," she said, tears falling. "You'll never see light again." Tejaswi was sentenced to life in prison, her ambition a shattered crown, her cries echoing as guards led her away.

Nyay, cleared of all charges, knelt before Devi in the palace's private garden, where roses bloomed despite the war's scars. His armor was gone, his kurta simple, his face etched with guilt. "I'm sorry, Mother," he said, tears falling. "I couldn't save Father, or Vishesh."

Devi pulled him into a hug, her sobs soft against his shoulder. "You're my son," she whispered. "That's enough." She cupped his face, her eyes warm. "Rule with your heart, Nyay. Break the curse."

He nodded, his resolve renewed. "For you, for Vishesh," he vowed, his voice steady.

In Bhaanugarh, the palace shimmered under a clear sky, its marble walls alive with celebration. The city's streets were lined with marigolds, their scent mingling with the smoke of sacred fires. Anokhi rode through the gates, her lehenga crimson, her bow at her side, her eyes wide with awe. The people cheered, calling her "Princess Anokhi," their voices a wave of love. Inderjeet, his face lined but radiant, stood at the palace steps, his arms open. "My daughter," he said, his voice breaking as he hugged her. "You're home."

Adhirath joined them, holding their mother's necklace, its lotus pendant gleaming. He placed it around Anokhi's neck, his eyes proud. "This was hers," he said softly. "You're home, sister."

Anokhi touched the pendant, tears falling. "I feel her," she whispered, her heart full. "Thank you, Adhirath."

That evening, a feast filled the palace, tables groaning with rice, curries, and sweets. Musicians played, their sitars weaving melodies of hope. Anokhi sat beside Nyay, who had ridden from Udaipur, his new crown simple but heavy. He leaned close, his voice low. "You're my queen, Anokhi," he said, his eyes shining. "Will you marry me?"

She smiled, her heart soaring. "Yes, palace boy," she said, her voice warm. "But I'm keeping my bow."

He laughed, kissing her hand, the crowd's cheers a joyful roar. Inderjeet raised a goblet, his voice strong. "To Anokhi, our princess, and Nyay, Udaipur's king. May their love heal our lands!"

The palace glowed, but in Rajgarh, Leela stood by Hari's grave, a letter from Anokhi in her hands. "I'm a princess, Ma," it read, "but you're my mother. Come to Bhaanugarh." Leela smiled, tears falling. "My brave girl," she whispered, the stars above her a testament to Anokhi's light.

In Udaipur's dungeon, Tejaswi sat alone, her silks replaced by coarse cloth, her dreams dust. She clutched a crumpled letter, her voice a whisper. "I could've been queen." But the bars were cold, her fate sealed.

Anokhi and Nyay stood on Bhaanugarh's balcony, the city's lights twinkling below. "We'll rule together," Nyay said, his arm around her. "No more curses, only love."

Anokhi nodded, her necklace glinting, her heart full. "For our families," she said, her voice a vow. "For our home."

The kingdoms of Bhaanugarh, Udaipur, and Rajgarh, once torn by betrayal, stood united under a new dawn. Anokhi, born to rule, had found her place—not just as a princess, but as a bridge between hearts, her courage a light that would shine for generations.

X

A New Dawn

Udaipur's palace glowed like a constellation, its sandstone walls adorned with thousands of clay lamps that flickered under a velvet sky. The air was alive with the scent of jasmine and rosewater, mingling with the rhythmic beat of dhol drums and the sweet strains of shehnai music. The grand courtyard, draped in crimson and gold silks, buzzed with the laughter of nobles, farmers, and merchants, their voices uniting in celebration. Nyay and Anokhi's wedding was a spectacle, a testament to love that had triumphed over war and betrayal, binding the kingdoms of Udaipur, Bhaanugarh, and Rajgarh.

Anokhi stood at the center of the mandap, her golden lehenga shimmering with intricate zari work, its heavy dupatta trailing like a river of light. Her hands, adorned with henna in swirling patterns, trembled slightly as she adjusted her maang tikka, its ruby catching the firelight. Nyay, beside her, was resplendent in a royal sherwani of ivory and gold, his turban crowned with a peacock feather. His eyes, warm and steady, never left her. "You're beautiful," he whispered, his voice soft amid the priest's chants.

Anokhi's cheeks flushed, her smile shy. "You're not so bad yourself, Palace boy," she teased, her voice trembling with joy.

Raja Dev Rana, seated near the sacred fire, performed the kanyadaan, his weathered hands gently placing Anokhi's in Nyay's. His eyes were misty, his silver hair glowing in the firelight. "You're my pride, Anokhi," he said, his voice thick with emotion. "Geetanjali would be so proud."

Anokhi's throat tightened, her fingers squeezing Dev's. "Thank you, Dada Maharaj," she whispered. "You made me a warrior."

The crowd erupted in cheers as Nyay tied the mangalsutra around her neck, its black beads a promise of forever. Petals rained from above, and the people of Udaipur shouted, "Long live King Nyay! Long live Queen Anokhi!" Adhirath, standing beside Inderjeet, clapped loudly, his heart full. He approached Anokhi after the ceremony, his necklace—twin to hers—glinting at his throat. "You're the sister I dreamed of," he said, pulling her into a hug. "Bhaanugarh's lucky to have you back."

Anokhi hugged him tightly, tears in her eyes. "And I'm lucky to have you, brother," she said, her voice warm. "We're family now."

The feast stretched into the night, tables groaning with platters of biryani, jalebis, and mango lassis. Leela, radiant in a new sari, sat beside Devi, their laughter a bridge between Rajgarh's fields and Udaipur's palace. "Your girl's a queen," Devi said, her eyes soft. "Hari's smiling from the stars."

Leela wiped a tear, her smile proud. "She's still my Anokhi," she said, watching her daughter dance with Nyay, their steps light despite the weight of their crowns.

Months later, Anokhi stood on the palace balcony, her hands resting on her gently swelling belly. The city's markets sparkled below, their stalls vibrant with silks and spices, a sign of Udaipur's newfound peace. Nyay joined her, his arm around her waist, his face glowing with quiet joy. "How's our little warrior?" he asked, his hand brushing her stomach.

Anokhi laughed, leaning into him. "Kicking like he's ready to rule," she said, her voice warm. "He's got your spirit."

Nyay's eyes softened. "And your courage. He'll be perfect."

Her pregnancy was a time of light and laughter, though not without challenges. Morning sickness kept her in bed some days, but Nyay was ever attentive, bringing her fresh fruits and telling stories of his childhood to make her smile. "Vishesh and I once stole a horse from the stables," he said, grinning as he sat by her bedside. "We thought we'd be knights."

Anokhi chuckled, her hand on his. "You're still a knight to me," she said, her eyes shining. "Just don't steal my horse."

Leela visited often, her hands busy knitting tiny clothes, her voice full of advice. "Rest, beta," she said, tucking a blanket around Anokhi. "This child's your heart now."

Anokhi hugged her, tears falling. "I miss Pitaji," she whispered. "He'd love this."

Leela's eyes glistened. "He's with you, always."

The palace staff adored Anokhi, their queen who still greeted them by name and shared mangoes in the kitchens. One evening, a young maid, Lila, shyly offered her a woven bracelet. "For the baby, Rani-ji," she said, blushing.

Anokhi's heart swelled, slipping it on. "It's beautiful, Lila," she said, her voice warm. "Uday will treasure it."

As her belly grew, so did Udaipur's prosperity. Nyay ruled justly, easing taxes and rebuilding villages scarred by Vishesh's reign. Anokhi, even heavy with child, rode through the city, her bow at her side, listening to the people's needs. "You're our heart, Rani-ji," an old farmer said, offering her a basket of guavas.

She smiled, accepting it. "And you're ours," she said, her voice firm. "We'll grow strong together."

The day of Uday's birth arrived under a clear dawn, the palace alive with anticipation. Anokhi labored in her chamber, its walls draped with soft blue silks, the air thick with the scent of rosewater. Midwives bustled, their voices calm, while Nyay paced outside, his heart pounding. "She's strong," he muttered, clutching a prayer bead. "She'll be fine."

A cry pierced the air, strong and vibrant. A midwife emerged, beaming. "A boy, Maharaj! Healthy and loud!" Nyay rushed in, tears streaming as he saw Anokhi, pale but radiant, cradling their son. Uday Pratap Singh, with his mother's fierce eyes and his father's gentle smile, cooed softly. "He's perfect," Nyay whispered, kissing Anokhi's forehead.

She smiled, exhausted but joyful. "Our light," she said, her voice soft. "Like you wished at the tree."

Nyay's heart swelled, the memory of his plea at the wish-granting tree—freedom from his father's shadow—now fulfilled. "The curse is broken," he said, his voice thick. "Because of you."

Years passed, and Uday's laughter filled Udaipur's palace, a melody that echoed through its halls. At three, he toddled through the gardens, chasing butterflies, his tiny sherwani smeared with mud. Anokhi ran after him, laughing. "Slow down, Uday!" she called, scooping him up. "You're faster than my horse!"

Nyay joined them, lifting Uday onto his shoulders. "He's a king already," he said, grinning. "Look at that smile."

Uday giggled, tugging Nyay's turban. "Papa, fly!" he squealed, and Nyay spun him, their laughter a beacon of joy.

Bhaanugarh and Udaipur flourished, their markets vibrant with trade, their fields lush with crops. Adhirath visited often, his rule in Bhaanugarh kind but firm. He brought Uday a wooden sword, laughing as the boy swung it wildly. "He's a warrior," Adhirath said, hugging Anokhi. "Like his mother."

She smiled, her necklace glinting. "And his uncle," she said, her voice warm. "You're family, Adhirath."

In Rajgarh, Dev, now frail but content, watched Uday play in the fields where Anokhi once worked. Leela sat beside him, her hair gray but her smile bright. "She's a queen," Dev said, his voice soft, "but she's still our girl."

Leela nodded, tears in her eyes. "Hari's proud, I know it."

Dev took Uday's hand, teaching him to plant a sapling. "Grow strong, little king," he said, his eyes misty. "Your mother was born to rule, and so are you."

That evening, Anokhi and Nyay stood on Udaipur's balcony, the city's lights twinkling below. Uday slept in their chamber, his tiny snores a quiet comfort. "We did it," Nyay said, his arm around Anokhi. "Peace, love, a family."

Anokhi leaned into him, her heart full. "We fought for it," she said, her voice steady. "For them, for us."

Nyay kissed her temple, his voice soft. "You're my queen, my warrior, my home."

She smiled, her eyes on the stars. "And you're my city boy, my king, my heart."

The kingdoms of Bhaanugarh, Udaipur, and Rajgarh stood united, their scars healed by love and justice. Anokhi, once a farmer's daughter, now a queen, had fulfilled her destiny, her courage a light that would guide Uday and generations to come. The wish-granting tree in Rajgarh's jungle stood silent, its threads fluttering, its magic complete.